Benji

BENJI MAKES THE TEAM

BENJI

Published by Scholastic Inc., *Publishers since 1920.* SCHOLASTIC and associated logos are trademarks and/or registered trademarks of Scholastic Inc.

The publisher does not have any control over and does not assume any responsibility for author or third-party websites or their content.

This book is a work of fiction. Names, characters, places, and incidents are either the product of the author's imagination or are used fictitiously, and any resemblance to actual persons, living or dead, business establishments, events, or locales is entirely coincidental.

ISBN 978-1-338-59019-7

10 9 8 7 6 5 4 3 2 1   20 21 22 23 24

Printed in the U.S.A.   40
First printing 2020

Benji

BENJI MAKES THE TEAM

by Mary Tillworth

Scholastic Inc.

CHAPTER 1

On a windless afternoon in a small town in the South, a golden-haired mutt came trotting into view. His head was bent to the ground as he sniffed. As usual, Benji was hunting for food.

His ears perked up as he picked up the faint scent of popcorn. Following his nose, Benji made his way to a set of metal bleachers next to a large field enclosed by a chain-link fence. Ducking under them, he found what he was looking for—a dropped bag of buttery popcorn lying in the dirt.

When he had crunched down the last popped kernel, Benji licked his lips happily. He came out from under the bleachers and was just about to keep on his way when he heard a loud crack of a ball hitting wood.

"Run, Brandon, run!" called a man wearing a

cap and holding a clipboard. Everyone in the bleachers stood up and cheered as a tall and thin boy with deep brown skin and short curly hair dropped his bat and began to hurtle toward first base.

Now that his belly was somewhat full, Benji looked around for the first time. The field was alive with middle school boys. Some hovered around the bases as Brandon tore his way across them, making the outline of a big diamond. Others were deeper in the field, looking up at a ball flying through the air. A short, redheaded kid wearing a blue-and-white-striped uniform reached up with a gloved hand and jumped, but he missed. The ball landed a few yards behind him. He scrambled to pick it up, and then threw it to a boy in the center of the field, who then threw the ball toward home plate. A kid with a black mask caught the ball, but not before Brandon had slid into the mat, kicking up a cloud of dust.

"Safe!" called the ump.

"Bran-don! Bran-don! Bran-don!" cried a group of kids from a dugout next to the field.

Benji woofed and wagged his tail. He wasn't sure why everyone seemed excited, but he liked happy kids. As he watched the ball game continue, he noticed a lone figure with long dark hair swept up in a tight ponytail. She was standing next to the fence at the far end of the field. Her hands were curled around the chain links and she was watching the game with fierce intensity. Benji noticed something else about her, too. Dangling halfway out of her pocket was a stick of beef jerky that made his mouth water.

Even though he was half full of popcorn, Benji never said no to the possibility of food. He made his way over to the girl and stood next to her, wagging his tail. The girl did not seem to notice. Her attention was riveted to the game being played on the other side of the fence.

Benji considered sneakily extracting the jerky from the girl's pocket, but he thought better of it. Instead, he nudged the girl's hand and gave a short bark.

Finally, the girl looked down. Her eyes widened in surprise. "*Hola, perrito,*" she said. "Are you watching the game, too?"

Benji cocked his head and looked steadily at the girl's pocket where the jerky piece was poking out.

"Ah, I see," the girl said with a laugh. "You don't care about this game—you just want my snack." She reached into her pocket and brought out the jerky. She bit off half of the stick, and then offered the rest of it to Benji. He scarfed it down in half a second.

The girl knelt in front of Benji. She wrinkled her nose. "Woo, you stink, perrito. You need a bath real bad." She checked around his neck. "And you've got no collar, too, which means you don't have a name. A stray, huh?"

Benji licked his chops and sat politely. His tail thumped happily against the ground.

"Well, *my* name is Gabriela. And you're one cute dog." The girl laughed. "Want to come and meet my family? The game's over so I should be going home anyway."

Benji lifted his eyebrows. He didn't know what Gabriela was saying, but he sensed that she was trying to make friends with him. His instinct was proven right when she took another piece of jerky that had been hidden in her pocket and waved it in front of him.

"*Vamos, perrito,*" said Gabriela. "When we get home, I'll see if there's any more food I can get for you." She held the jerky by her knees and began to walk.

Benji followed, sniffing at the treat just a few feet ahead of him. When they had gone down the length of the field and reached the dugout, the girl stopped and let him have the jerky.

As Benji munched on his second treat, the kid Brandon appeared from the dugout, carrying a bat and his mitt. He was the only player left on the ball field.

"Nice home run," called Gabriela.

Brandon stopped. "Do I know you?" he asked.

Gabriela shook her head. "Nah. But I watch your games here all the time. You're really good!"

Brandon shrugged. "I know," he said. "No one can slug it out of the park like me."

"You know, I play ball with my brother sometimes," said Gabriela. "I can hit pretty hard. And I can pitch, too."

Brandon laughed. "Yeah, but you're a girl. You're never gonna play as hard as us guys."

Gabriela folded her arms. "Maybe it's because I've never been given the chance!"

"Yeah, well, we've got tryouts next Wednesday because one of our players is moving to Canada," said Brandon. "Why don't you see if you've got what it takes to join the Tigers?"

"I would love that!" shouted Gabriela.

Brandon laughed. "Just kidding. You have to be a boy to try out."

"Says who?" demanded Gabriela.

"Says life," retorted Brandon. "Now if you'll excuse me, I have to go home and update my home run stats. Another season like this, and I'm headed for varsity next year." He slung the bat over his shoulder and walked away.

Gabriela watched him go. "He thinks he's such a hotshot," she fumed. "I bet I could out-bat him any day!"

Benji was only half paying attention. Once again,

he was distracted by the tantalizing smell of food—this time coming from the empty dugout. His hungry nose led him to a few forgotten baseballs and a stray bat lying underneath a wooden bench. Behind the bat was a half-eaten granola bar that had fallen into the dirt. Benji scooped it up in his mouth and gulped. The granola bar disappeared down his throat.

When he lifted his head from under the bench, Gabriela was picking up the bat. Baseballs bulged from her pockets. Benji followed her to the place where Brandon had slid into the mat.

Gabriela rummaged through her pocket and took out a baseball. She tossed it high in the air. She stepped back and swung. Benji heard a terrific crack, and the ball flew up through the air, soaring higher and faster than the ball that earned Brandon his home run.

Benji looked over at Gabriela. Her face was a mask of determination, but there was a glint of sheer happiness on her face that she couldn't hide. Benji didn't know what Gabriela was doing, but she looked so natural standing by the home plate, her ponytail whipping against her back as she took another ball and slugged it deep into the outfield.

Benji had an idea. He galloped onto the grass and rooted around until he came upon the ball that Gabriela had sent flying. He picked it up in his mouth and returned it to her. Then he did the same with the second baseball.

Gabriela smiled down at him. "Hey, thanks for being my ball boy!" Her eyebrows lifted with excitement. "You know what? Maybe I *will* try out for the team next week. And you can help me practice!"

Benji woofed. As Gabriela continued to practice her swing, he leapt out to retrieve ball after ball. It was only when the sun was setting that Gabriela stopped. She went into the dugout and returned the bat and the balls. Then she waved a hand at Benji.

"Come on, perrito," she said. "Let's go home."

Before he fell in line behind Gabriela, Benji darted into the dugout and clamped his teeth down on one of the baseballs. He knew it brought her a lot of joy, and he was going to bring it wherever she was.

CHAPTER 2

Holding the baseball in his mouth, Benji walked with Gabriela past the field and down a road that led toward the center of the town. Gabriela led him to a cozy split-level house with tomatoes and cilantro growing in a small garden bed in the front yard. She trotted up the front porch and opened the door. "Mami, I'm home!" she called.

"Ay, *mi amor*, where were you?" A tall woman with dark eyes and streaks of gray in her tightly braided hair came out. She looked down at Benji. "And who is this?"

"I was watching the ball game." Gabriela knelt down and scratched Benji's head. "And this is, um, Perrito. He followed me home. Can we give him dinner?"

Mami sighed. "*Sí, sí,* you know I can't refuse an animal in need. He can have some food after you give him a bath." She raised her eyebrows. "Gabriela, baseball games don't go so late. Were you out there trying to play ball again?"

"Well . . . yes," said Gabriela. She rushed on. "Mami, they're having tryouts next Wednesday and I think I can make the team. I've been practicing with Jorge and he says I'm really good!"

Mami frowned. "Your brother shouldn't be putting ideas into your head. Jorge knows that baseball is for the boys."

"Baseball is for anybody who's good enough to play it!" protested Gabriela.

Mami shook her head. "Gabriela, why do you insist on making things so difficult for yourself? Instead of sliding around in the dirt, you could be doing something beautiful. Like ballet."

Gabriela groaned. "Mami, for the last time, I don't want to do ballet! I know you loved being a ballerina and performing around the world, but I want to be slamming balls out of the park, not standing on my tiptoes in a tutu!"

"But, Gabriela, you have such great promise! Remember the dance recitals you did in elementary school? You were in the center every single time because you were the best."

"Sí, Mami, I know I was good at it. But ballet

doesn't make me feel alive the way that baseball does," said Gabriela.

Benji could tell that Gabriela and her mom were getting frustrated with each other. To distract them, he dropped the baseball and nudged it toward Gabriela's feet.

Even though her face had turned red, Gabriela laughed when she saw Benji nosing the ball toward her. She reached down and picked up the ball. She tossed it in the air, her wrist flicking it up, and caught it easily. "When I'm on the field, I feel more like myself than any other time."

"I do not understand your love of baseball, and you do not understand how magnificent ballet can be," said Mami. "But if you change your mind, there are auditions for an advanced class with Madame Miyoko next month. My old barre is still in the basement. I can help you practice."

"Mami, you haven't been listening," Gabriela said with a sigh. "I'm going to give Perrito a hose-down in the backyard. And when I come in for dinner, please let's not talk about baseball or ballet or anything else that begins with a *b*."

"All right, mi amor," said Mami. "Dinner is in half an hour. Make sure that dog is nice and clean before he comes into the house."

"Wait here a second, Perrito," said Gabriela. "I've got to get some shampoo from the bathroom."

As Gabriela disappeared into the house, Mami bent down and gave Benji a scratch underneath his chin. Her mouth curled into a smile. "You remind me of my childhood dog. He came off the streets, just like you. He was tough. He knew who he was. Unlike some daughters who still need to figure that out."

Benji nuzzled his chin into Mami's hand, letting her scratch deeper. Even though she had raised her voice with Gabriela, he could tell that she loved her daughter very much.

Gabriela reappeared holding a large plastic bottle and a towel. "Vamos," she told Benji.

Benji hopped off the porch and went with Gabriela around the house to a long, narrow backyard. Gabriela turned on a spigot, and clear cold water began to gush from a garden hose snaking across the grass.

Gabriela grabbed the hose and began to pour water over Benji. He waited patiently as she poured shampoo onto his grimy fur and worked it into a thick lather. After she had rinsed him off, he was several shades lighter than he had been that morning. He braced himself and shook vigorously, sending droplets of water flying everywhere.

Gabriela laughed. She unfolded the towel and flung it over Benji's torso. After rubbing him dry, she crouched down and gave his neck a good sniff. "Much better," she declared.

"Hey, Gabby, dinner's ready!" A lean boy wearing faded jeans and a backward cap on his head went up to Benji. "Mami know about this guy?"

Gabriela nodded. "You know she has a soft spot for strays." She stood up. "Hey, Jorge, do you think I'm good enough to make the middle school baseball team?"

Jorge shrugged. "Sure you are. You can hit the ball farther than most guys in high school I know. Plus, you've got a killer arm. With a little pitching practice, you could be deadly on the field."

"The team is having tryouts next Wednesday. Do you think you could help me practice?"

"I could. But I don't think Coach Stevens would let you try out because . . . well, because you're a girl."

Benji watched Gabriela's face become clouded over. Then, as if a switch had been flipped, it lit up.

"Maybe he doesn't have to know that I'm a girl," she said.

"What do you mean?" asked Jorge.

"Never mind," said Gabriela. "Just say you'll help me practice, and I'll take care of Coach Stevens and his old-fashioned ways myself."

"Anything for my favorite sister," said Jorge.

"I'm your *only* sister," said Gabriela.

Jorge smiled. "Just be glad you don't have competition. Now let's go inside. I'm so hungry, my stomach is growling."

That night Benji curled up at the foot of Gabriela's bed with a belly full of rice and chicken. The baseball he had brought from the field was resting two feet above his head, tucked into Gabriela's pitching hand.

CHAPTER 3

After breakfast the next morning, Benji accompanied Gabriela to the baseball diamond. Jorge came with them, bringing a catcher's mask, a chest protector, kneepads, and two worn mitts. When they arrived at the ball field, it was deserted.

Jorge yawned. "It's so early, Gabriela. Are you sure we need to practice at six in the morning?"

"No one on the baseball team can see me," said Gabriela. "Not if my plan is going to work."

Jorge put on his equipment and tossed Gabriela a mitt. "Are you sure you don't want to tell me about your plan?"

Gabriela caught the mitt and slipped it over her hand. "I'm sure. Now, get ready to catch some fastballs."

Benji watched, fascinated, as Gabriela threw the ball to Jorge over and over. Her pitches were so fast, the ball seemed to smoke. But half the time it flew so far away from Jorge that he had to leap in the air or lunge sideways to get it.

The hundredth time Jorge had to jump to catch the ball, he held on to it instead of throwing it back to Gabriela. "Gabby, we both know you can pitch fast. But you've got to concentrate on your aim. Your arm is useless if the ball doesn't fly into the hitting zone."

"Fine," said Gabriela. "I'll just pretend that the hitting zone is one big square tutu."

An hour later, Jorge stood up. "Much better," he announced.

"Thanks," said Gabriela.

"I don't think you need to work on hitting—you've already got that down," said Jorge. "But how are you in the outfield?"

"Let's find out." Gabriela left the pitcher's mound and jogged away from home plate. When she was deep in center field, she turned around and bent her knees. She clapped a fist into her mitt. "Ready!" she shouted.

Benji watched as Jorge cracked a ball into the outfield. As Gabriela ran and leapt to catch it, Benji saw the smooth flow of her movements and the nimble power coursing through her body. She was like a gazelle, moving with easy grace. He barked happily when she lifted her arm and the ball smacked into her open mitt.

"Nice catch!" Jorge called as Gabriela threw the ball back to him. He paused. "I hate to say it, but Mami's right. You could be a dancer, too, if you wanted."

Gabriela's face darkened. "Don't you even begin . . ."

Jorge held up a hand. "Gabby, I'm not saying you shouldn't play ball. What I'm saying is that maybe you could do both. You know that professional football players take ballet, don't you?"

"Just hit the ball!" demanded Gabriela.

"Okay, okay," said Jorge. He threw the ball up and hit it into the outfield again.

After another hour, Jorge set down the bat and wiped his brow. "Gabby, I'm done for the day. I'm going home to wash up."

"I'll be there soon," Gabriela said. "Leave the bat." She ran up to Benji and scratched behind his ears. "Ready to fetch, Perrito?"

Benji woofed and jumped up, licking Gabriela's face.

Gabriela laughed. "You're a good dog." She jogged to the bat and picked it up. She took the baseball and flung it high in the air as Benji ran into the outfield, ready to bring the ball back to her when it came his way.

By the time Gabriela and Benji made their way back to the house, Benji's tongue hung from his mouth and his tail was only at half-mast. He had chased the baseball all morning and was ready for some down-time. After feeding him a snack and putting a big bowl of cold water out for him to drink, Gabriela left him in the backyard, where he padded around in half a dozen circles before flopping down for a well-earned nap.

He woke to the sound of a door opening. His mouth opened in a giant yawn as he got to his feet and walked to the front porch.

Gabriela was heading down the steps. Her long, flowing hair was pinned into an impossibly small bun at the top of her head. When she saw Benji, she shook her head. "I'm going shopping, Perrito. You've got to stay here."

Benji could tell by Gabriela's tone that she wanted him to stay. Still, he stayed at her heels as she strode along the sidewalk. There was a steely look on her face, and he knew that she was about to do some-thing that was very important to her. He wanted to be around to see it.

Gabriela headed into a busy part of town where

shops lined either side of the street. She stopped in front of a small door painted bright lavender with a turquoise knob. Through the storefront window Benji could see brightly colored costumes.

Gabriela looked down at Benji. "Stay, Perrito," she commanded.

Benji sat. He watched Gabriela take a deep breath before twisting the doorknob and going inside.

Out in the field, Gabriela had looked so sure of herself. Now Benji could see that she was really nervous. She studied the front of the store, then disappeared deeper into the shop.

Benji waited, but after a couple minutes his curiosity got the best of him. When the next customer opened the door, he slipped inside and went looking for Gabriela.

He found her in the back, looking at a wall covered with mannequin heads. Perched on top of each smooth head was a wig. There were at least fifty of them, brown and black and red and even blue, with some as long as Gabriela's hair.

Benji studied Gabriela's face. She looked disappointed. As she walked up and down the aisle, she kept shaking her head. "None of these are short enough," she muttered to herself.

Benji was only half listening. His nose had caught the scent of something fruity and delicious. He followed it to a large wooden box at the other end of the store. The smell was coming from the bottom of the box.

Benji turned his head from side to side to make sure no one was looking. Then he hopped into the box and began to dig. Hats and scarves and pieces of hair flew out from under his paws.

"Who let a dog inside this store!" yelled an angry voice.

"Perrito! What are you doing!" yelped Gabriela.

Benji emerged from the box triumphantly holding a wig in his mouth. It was strawberry blond and very short.

Gabriela pried the wig out from Benji's clenched teeth. She sniffed it. "Smells like someone poured fruit shampoo all over this," she said. "I know you think it's food, Perrito, but it's not."

A stern-looking man with thick glasses rushed up to them. "Did your dog just chomp on that wig?"

Benji wagged his tail. He jumped out of the box and tried to look as apologetic as possible.

"Yeah, he did," said Gabriela. She held the wig up to give it to the man, but then stopped. "How much is it?" she asked him.

The man motioned toward the box. "This is the bargain bin. Everything's seventy-five percent off the price tag."

Gabriela glanced at the worn paper tag attached

to the wig with a bit of yarn. "Ten bucks, huh?" she said. She went over to a full-length mirror next to a changing room. She fitted the wig over her head and tucked her hair underneath it.

Benji barked, confused. With the wig on, Gabriela looked like a completely different person. If she had just been walking down the street, he wouldn't have recognized her.

Gabriela took the wig off and smiled. "It's perfect. I'll take it," she told the shop owner.

"Good," he said. "And make sure that dog doesn't go rooting around the bargain bin. He shouldn't be in here in the first place."

Gabriela hastily paid for the wig and escorted Benji out of the shop. Once they were back in the sunlight, she gave him a big hug. "Thanks for finding this for me. I think you're pretty good luck," she told him. "Now we just need to hope that my disguise works on Wednesday."

CHAPTER 4

As the week rolled by, Benji went to the ball field with Gabriela early in the morning before school started. Jorge had been there once or twice more, but on the other days, Benji had helped Gabriela practice ball by himself. He loved watching her play, her long hair swinging in the sunlight as she ripped the ball into the air with sheer ferocity and joy. He wasn't able to catch for her when she pitched, but he learned from her facial expressions that she was aiming for the two feet of space above the home plate.

Then there came the day when Gabriela made twenty blisteringly fast throws, one after another, each flying exactly two feet over the center of home plate. When she had thrown the twentieth pitch, Gabriela turned to Benji, her face flushed, and broke out in a grin so big it seemed to stretch from one end of the field to the other.

Benji tilted his head back and howled his approval. Whatever Gabriela was preparing for, she was ready.

The next morning, Gabriela didn't go to the field as usual. Instead, she woke up an hour past the sun, and only had time to dress and eat breakfast before she ran off to school. When she returned in the afternoon, Benji was waiting for her with the baseball in his mouth.

But instead of calling him to follow her to the field, Gabriela went up to her room. Benji went along with her. He watched as she took the strawberry-blond wig out from under her mattress and fixed it over her coiled-up hair with dozens of bobby pins. When she was done, she went to a mirror hanging on her bedroom door and stared into it. She shook her head hard from side to side, then bopped it up and down as though she was rocking out to a heavy-metal song.

The wig did not budge. Satisfied, Gabriela tucked a stray wisp of her real hair firmly underneath and headed out the door with Benji at her heels.

When they reached the ball field, there were over a dozen boys waiting by the bleachers. The man with the clipboard Benji had seen on his first day in the town was there, writing down their names.

Gabriela walked up to him. "Coach Stevens, I'd like to try out for the school baseball team."

Coach Stevens looked up from his clipboard. He stared hard at Gabriela.

From the bleachers, Benji could see Gabriela's face turn pale. She swallowed hard.

"Name?" barked Coach Stevens.

Gabriela's eyes lit up. "Gabrielaaa . . . aah, my name is, aah, Gabriel Lopez. Gabe for short."

"You new here? I haven't seen you around or at the school," said Coach Stevens.

"Yeah. Just moved to town a week ago. And I'm homeschooled, which is why you haven't seen me," said Gabriela. Her hands curled into tight fists and she bit her lip.

"Well, Gabe, there are twelve other boys waiting to try out for the team. You're lucky number thirteen," said Coach Stevens. "Wait in the bleachers until I call your name."

"Yes, Coach!" chirped Gabriela. She left the field and ran toward Benji, her face aglow. "He believed my disguise!" she whispered as she ruffled his fur.

Benji dropped the baseball he had been holding and reached up and licked Gabriela's fingers. He could feel her nervousness in the way her hand trembled. He picked the baseball back up and dropped it into her hand. It was worn and covered in slobber, but it was also a reminder of all the days they had spent practicing, getting her batting and pitching and fielding into shape.

Gabriela flipped the ball high in the air and caught it with her other hand. She smiled at Benji. "You're right. I have been working hard. I shouldn't be scared—I should be excited."

But when Coach Stevens called her name, Gabriela couldn't stop shaking. She kept touching her wig and Benji realized that she was so worried about getting found out, she couldn't concentrate. At bat, she let easy balls go by and only managed to hit two into the infield. When she was in the outfield, wind would blow through her fake hair and she would clamp her mitt to her head instead of catching the ball.

Benji watched Gabriela, but he watched Coach Stevens as well. He saw the coach shaking his head as he scribbled down notes about Gabriela.

Benji knew Gabriela would have to wow the coach with her throwing arm if she was going to make the team. As she approached the pitcher's mound, Benji trotted to the edge of the fence. Just before Gabriela wound up for her first pitch, he drew back his head. A magnificent howl burst from his throat, as loud and as joyful as the day when he had seen Gabriela throw twenty perfect pitches.

Gabriela paused. She looked at Benji as he crooned his pride and his encouragement to her. The worry creasing her forehead disappeared. She drew back, pulled the ball from her mitt, and then lunged forward.

The ball flew straight and true, right into the catcher's outstretched mitt.

The catcher yelped and stood up, pulling his hand out of his glove and shaking it out. "Ow, that hurt!" he yelled.

The pen dropped from Coach Stevens's hand. His jaw hung open.

The catcher threw the ball back to Gabriela. She wound up and threw another blazingly perfect pitch.

"Do that again," said Coach Stevens.

Gabriela did it again.

"I'm going to need a thicker mitt," moaned the catcher.

At the end of another ten pitches, Coach Stevens had made up his mind. "Gabe, welcome to the team," he said. "With you pitching, we could make it to the championships."

Gabriela flung her arms up into the air. "I'll help us get there, Coach, I promise," she said.

Later that afternoon, as Gabriela and Benji were walking home, Gabriela made a detour to the local pet store and bought a bag of jerky snacks. She sat on a bench and tossed them, one by one, to Benji, who happily caught them in his mouth.

"Thanks for howling at me today," said Gabriela.

"I felt like such a different person with my wig on that I couldn't focus on the game. You reminded me to be myself. And being myself means loving baseball and throwing as hard as I can."

Benji jumped up on the bench and gave Gabriela a huge kiss on her cheek. He could tell she was happy. All her fear was gone.

Gabriela looked at Benji thoughtfully. "You're completely yourself, too, Perrito. You've got an awesome personality. You're smart, and tough, and can make me smile when no one else can. And it doesn't matter that you're a stray mutt—you're the coolest dog I know. In fact, I bet it's because you've seen a lot of ups and downs in your life that you're the way you are. I wouldn't trade you for the fanciest purebred in the world."

Benji laid his head on Gabriela's knee. This time when he licked her salty fingers, they were calm and strong and sure. He was glad that he had helped to get them that way.

CHAPTER 5

When Gabriela showed up for her first Tigers home game with her strawberry-blond wig clamped tightly onto her head, Benji was right there in the stands, howling as she whacked baseballs out of the park and cranked out fastball after fastball.

At the end of the ninth inning, it was Tigers: 7, Fireflies: 0.

"Nice work," Brandon told Gabriela in the dugout as the players packed up to head home. "You're a natural on the field. I'm so glad you joined the team."

"Thanks," said Gabriela.

"Hey." Brandon frowned. "Are you sure we haven't met before? I swear your face looks familiar."

"Uh, I g-get that a lot," stammered Gabriela. "I have a really ordinary face—people always mistake me for someone else."

Brandon studied Gabriela closely. "No, that's not it. But . . ." He shook his head. "Never mind. You remind me of someone I met. But she was a girl."

Gabriela laughed nervously. "Well, we're definitely not the same person."

"Yeah, I guess so." Brandon shrugged. "Anyway, I'm heading home. Good game, Lopez." He held up his hand for a slap.

Gabriela high-fived Brandon. After Brandon had left, Benji trotted into the dugout. Gabriela adjusted her wig one last time. "*Vamos a la casa, Perrito,*" she told him.

As they walked home, Gabriela kept rubbing her shoulders. "Wow, I'm sore," she groaned. "Maybe a hot shower will help." When they reached the house, Gabriela left Benji in the living room. "I'm gonna be a while," she told Benji as she closed the bathroom door.

A few minutes later, over the hiss of running water, Benji heard music playing. It was coming from underneath him.

Curious, Benji went over to the basement door and nudged it open. He walked down the steps and saw Gabriela's mom standing at a barre. She was wearing a black leotard, tan tights, and pink slippers of some kind. Her dark hair was neatly pinned up in a bun. There was a wall of mirrors next to the barre.

There was an old record player in the corner. Music sprang from it. Benji watched as Mami swept her arms and her legs in smooth, practiced arcs. Elegance seemed to flow out of her softly curled fingers and sharply pointed toes.

As she moved, Benji was reminded of Gabriela. The two women were so alike in their power and grace.

Up on the main level of the house, he heard Gabriela calling him. Benji woofed and woofed until Gabriela's face appeared at the top of the basement stairs.

"There you are, Perrito!" Gabriela came down the steps rubbing her hair with a towel. She wore leggings and a loose T-shirt—Benji had stayed with her long enough to know that they would most likely become her pajamas that night. She had been practicing so hard, she often fell asleep exhausted without changing into her real pajamas.

Gabriela stopped when she saw her mother at the barre. "Mami, what are you doing?" she asked.

"Just moving my body around," said Mami. "I've been stooped over all day working in the garden and all my muscles are aching. I need to loosen my limbs and stretch."

Gabriela rubbed her shoulder. "Does it make you less sore?"

"*Sí, claro que sí*," said Mami.

Gabriela hesitated, then draped the towel over the banister. "Can I join you?"

Mami smiled. "Of course!"

Gabriela took a spot at the barre behind Mami. "*Lista, Mami,*" she said. "I'm ready."

"Follow the music, and follow me," said Mami. She pointed her feet away from each other and lifted her arm above her head. She bent her knees into a plié. "First." She pointed out a foot and settled into a wide stance as her arm fell to her side. She pliéd. "Second." Her arm swept back up and her foot crossed halfway in front of the other. Another plié. "Third." Her toe pointed in front of her. Plié. "Fourth." Finally, she matched one foot against the other and pliéd. "Fifth."

Benji watched Gabriela as she moved with her mother. Gabriela was great at baseball, but she looked like she was just as good at ballet.

After a series of exercises, Mami led Gabriela to the floor, where they stretched for a long, long time. Once they were done, Mami went over to the record player and switched it off.

"*Gracias, Mami,*" said Gabriela. "I do feel much better."

"How come you're so sore, mi amor?" Mami asked.

Gabriela turned red. "Uh, just gym class," she muttered.

Mami tsked. "They shouldn't make you run

around so much." She climbed up the stairs. "Ay, it's late. I need to make dinner."

"I'll help, Mami," said Gabriela. As she went up after her mom, Benji stayed in the basement and looked around. He saw the worn smoothness of the barre, the scuffs and marks across the wooden floor from countless sweeps of the foot. He could tell that Mami loved this place, and had poured her heart into the little practices that she and Gabriela had just shared.

Benji thought back to the argument Gabriela had had with her mom a week ago. Instinct told him that it had to do with Gabriela loving baseball, and Mami loving ballet. Baseball and ballet were very different. But Benji knew that if Gabriela could see how special ballet was to Mami, and Mami could see how dedicated Gabriela was to baseball, they would be able to figure out that they were both rooting for the same thing—a love of something that made them both feel most alive, and most themselves.

CHAPTER 6

Over the next month, Gabriela kept showing up to ball games with her strawberry-blond wig and her dynamite throwing arm, and the Tigers kept winning.

Tigers: 12, Coyotes: 2
Tigers: 8, Eagles: 4
Tigers: 9, Blue Birds: 0
Tigers: 6, Sharks: 3
Tigers: 4, Hornets: 3

The last team the Tigers played, the Hornets, had won the state championships last year. They had some ace batters and had nearly won with a grand slam in the ninth inning. Gabriela had stayed cool and shut out the last batter with three swift, sure fastballs. When the final out had been called, the entire team had rushed onto the field for a group hug.

"Great job, Gabe," said Coach Stevens. "Next game tomorrow is the semifinals. You keep pitching that way, and we're going to the state championships this year!"

That evening, Gabriela headed down into the basement. After every game she had made a habit of joining her mother at the barre to help her stretch and wind down.

Benji had noticed that the more time Gabriela spent with her mom practicing ballet, the better at baseball she seemed to become. Her pitches got even faster, and when she leapt to catch the ball, it was higher than she had ever jumped before. She was also slamming the ball so far down the field, in each game she almost always had one or two home runs.

As they were doing their final stretch, Mami looked over to Gabriela. "You know, mi amor, Madame Miyoko's ballet audition is tomorrow afternoon. I think you should go."

"I can't, Mami." Gabriela rose from the floor.

"Why not?" asked Mami. "You've been practicing with me all this time. I know talent when I see it. You're good, Gabriela Maria Elena Lopez. Very good."

Gabriela took a deep breath. "I appreciate you helping me stretch, but, Mami . . . the reason why I've been doing ballet with you is because I'm on the baseball team. After every game, I needed a way to stretch. So I came down here and joined you."

All the color fled from Mami's face. She stood up very slowly. "Do you mean to tell me that you are not interested in ballet at all? That all you care about is baseball? That all the hours I have been training you have been for nothing?" Her lips pinched together with anger and confusion. "How did you even make the team? You're a *girl*, Gabriela. No other girl I have ever heard of has played baseball."

"Well, you're looking at one now, even if I have to be in disguise," declared Gabriela. "I've been pretending to be a boy by wearing a wig I picked up in the costume shop last month. It has worked so far. And I can't go to Madame Miyoko's audition tomorrow because the semifinals are tomorrow. If we win this game, we go on to the state championships!" She went up to her mother and stared her directly in the eyes. "Please, Mami. I've been practicing really hard. The team needs me. And I want this more than anything I've ever wanted in my whole life."

Mami shook her head. "Do not speak to me of want. I see your talent. I see what you can become as a ballerina and my greatest desire is for you to realize your potential. But if you want to waste your talent chasing some stupid ball, then go ahead. But if you do not go to Madame Miyoko's audition tomorrow, I am never giving you another ballet lesson again."

"Fine!" shouted Gabriela. "I never want to take another lesson with you again, anyway!" She turned from her mom and fled up the stairs. Benji raced after her. He managed to slip into her room just before she slammed the door as hard as she could. She sat on the bed and put her head in her hands.

Benji hopped on the bed next to her. At first he just lay still as Gabriela wrapped her arms around him and hugged him tightly. Then he reached out and licked the salt off her face.

Gabriela smiled through her tears. "Hey, Perrito." She gently stroked Benji's fur. "Thanks for being here for me. Even if my mom can't be."

The next afternoon, Gabriela put on her wig and she and Benji left the house for the semifinal game. Halfway there, Benji realized he had forgotten the ball that he had carried to every one of Gabriela's games. It was the ball he had first fetched for her. It was the ball that had started the whole thing and given Gabriela hope. It was their lucky ball.

He had to go back for it. Benji barked and whined at Gabriela, and then started to head back to the house.

"Perrito, I'm going to be late for the game if I follow you. Catch up with me later," said Gabriela. She continued striding toward the field as Benji retraced his steps. When he reached Gabriela's house, he trotted up the front porch steps and whined and scratched at the door until Mami opened it.

"Ay, Perrito, do you know where Gabriela is?" Mami hunched down and patted Benji's head. "The audition is in an hour and I need to find her. I know she doesn't want to go, but it would be best for her."

Benji didn't know what Gabriela's mom was saying, but he was on a mission. He retrieved the beaten-up ball from Gabriela's room and started to trot down the street. When he looked behind him, Mami was following.

They made it to the ball field just as the second inning was starting. Benji guided Mami to the bleachers and they both sat down.

Mami gasped when she saw Gabriela, sporting bright blond hair, take the pitcher's mound. "My Gabriela is the *pitcher*?" she wondered.

Gabriela wound up and delivered a curveball that arced like lightning into the catcher's mitt. Time and time again, she threw the ball, and time again, the ump called batters out.

As Gabriela played, Benji watched Mami. He saw her face change from anger, to surprise, to pride. "My girl really can play," she said softly.

Benji nuzzled up to Mami. He dropped the ball into her lap. Mami picked it up and looked at it. "This ball has seen a lot of love. Is this what you used to practice with Gabriela?"

Benji woofed.

Mami nodded. "She has worked hard for this, hasn't she?"

Benji woofed again.

The semifinal game was hard fought, but in the end, the Tigers edged the Wolverines by one run, 3–2. As the players congratulated one another in the dugout, Mami went up to Coach Stevens. He was standing next to the home plate. "You have a great team," she told him.

"Thanks," said Coach Stevens. "Our newest addition has really been smoking it out of the ballpark."

"You mean Gabriela?" asked Mami.

Coach Stevens frowned. "Gabriela? No, I mean Gabe. Who's Gabriela?"

"Mami, what are you doing here?" Gabriela came out of the dugout, her mouth open. For the first time, Benji saw that her wig wasn't quite fastened onto her head. A few tufts of dark curly hair peeked out from under her temples.

"What happened to your hair?" Brandon came up behind Gabriela.

Gabriela reached up and touched her wig. As she did, a bobby pin fell to the ground. Another chunk of hair peeked out from underneath the wig.

"What's going on?" demanded Coach Stevens.

Gabriela tried to push her hair underneath the

wig, but all of a sudden a few more bobby pins gave way, and her long dark hair tumbled down.

"You're a girl?" gasped Brandon.

Coach Stevens raised his eyebrows. "You're a girl."

"I know. I'm sorry." Tears formed in Gabriela's eyes. Before they could fall down her cheeks, she turned and ran down the street, back toward her home.

Coach Stevens shook his head. "I can't let a girl play in the finals! What would the other coaches think?"

Mami stood in front of the coach. She raised her voice. "It doesn't matter what they think. What matters is that your best player is my daughter. If you don't let her play this game, you are throwing away that girl's dreams—and the championships."

"She's right," said Brandon. "I remember now. Gabriela was at the ball field last month. Only, she didn't have a wig on." He turned to Coach Stevens. "Coach, Gabriela's good. You know she is. You gotta let her play. It doesn't matter if she's a girl; she's part of our team."

Benji went up to Coach Stevens. He had the worn baseball in his mouth. He dropped it at the coach's feet.

Coach Stevens stooped down and picked it up. He looked at the worn stitches and the bite marks that peppered the tough leather. "All right," he said. "She can play. But she has to wear the wig and pretend to be a boy."

Mami shook her head. "No wig. My Gabriela is a girl and the best baseball player you will ever coach. You have no right to force her to pretend to be something she isn't."

"She's right, Coach," said Brandon. "And there's no written rule that the team has to be all boys."

Coach Stevens sighed. "No wig, then. But we'd better win the championship next week."

Mami grinned. "With my Gabriela on the team, you will."

CHAPTER 7

When Mami and Benji returned home, Benji was still carrying the lucky baseball. Gabriela's bedroom door was closed. Mami went up to it and knocked softly. "Mi amor, are you there?"

"Go away!" cried Gabriela.

"Gabriela, I talked to your coach. Everything is okay. You are going to play in the championships next week," said Mami.

There was a long pause. Then the door opened and Gabriela's face appeared. "What do you mean? Coach Stevens would never let a girl play on his team."

"Well, we convinced him otherwise," said Mami.

"But, Mami, you hate the fact that I play baseball! Why did you fight for me?" asked Gabriela.

Benji nosed his way into the room. He jumped on Gabriela's bed and pawed at the blanket. He woofed and sat down. The lucky baseball dropped from his mouth and rolled onto the floor.

Gabriela went to Benji and sat down. She stroked his fur as Mami joined her.

"I know you told me how much you loved baseball, but I wasn't listening to what you said. But when Perrito brought me to the ball game, I got to see how much you loved it. There was a fire in your eyes that reminded me of when I was a young ballerina, training every day to do the thing I loved."

Mami laid her hand on top of Gabriela's. "When I saw that fire, I knew I had to do something. And so your teammate Brandon and I convinced Coach Stevens to let you play in the championships. Without that ridiculous wig, too. You are a natural player, Gabriela. And you are a girl. And those are both fine. You should not have to pretend to be someone you're not."

Gabriela wiped her tears and smiled. "Gracias, Mami. Gracias." She took a deep breath. "I have to tell you something. I . . . I don't hate ballet. These past couple weeks practicing with you in the basement have been great. I like the way my body feels when I'm doing the exercises. I just didn't want you to think that I could care about ballet more than baseball." She hung her head. "And I'm sorry I missed Madame Miyoko's audition. I know it was today, and I actually thought about going. Doing ballet helps me be a better baseball player—but I like doing it just because, too."

"Tell you what, mi amor," said Mami. "I'll talk to Madame Miyoko and see if she can arrange a private audition for you. Would you like that?"

For a second, Gabriela hesitated. Then she reached over and hugged Mami. "Yes, Mami, I would like that very much."

"*Bueno*." Mami leaned down and picked up the fallen baseball. "In the meantime, I want you practicing for the big game next week." She handed it to Gabriela. "*Vamos, chica!* There is work to be done!"

Gabriela hopped off the bed and beckoned for Benji to join her. "Come on, Perrito. We can still hit a few balls before dark."

A few days later, Gabriela stood nervously at the barre of an elegant studio with worn hardwood floors and mirrors covering the length of one wall. Sunlight poured in from a large set of full-length windows, catching the highlights in her neatly pinned hair. She wore a simple black leotard and tights.

A slender woman with stern lines around her eyes and straight black hair bound in a perfect bun lifted the needle of a record player. "Ready, Gabriela?"

"Ready, Madame Miyoko," said Gabriela.

"I want you to go through all five positions in time with the music. Then we will go through a series of pirouettes, bourrées, and grands jetés," said Madame Miyoko. "And I want you to know that I am expecting a perfect performance. I do not do second auditions for my advanced ballet class, but because I respect your mother very much, I am giving you a chance."

"Thank you, Madame Miyoko," said Gabriela. "I will try not to disappoint you—or my mother."

From the corner of the studio, Mami smiled at her daughter. "You have never been a disappointment to me, mi amor," she told Gabriela.

As Madame Miyoko set the needle down, classical music filled the studio. Outside, Benji watched through the window as Gabriela began her exercises. After the barre, Madame Miyoko coached her through harder and harder moves, until Gabriela was spinning and leaping through the air. Her lips were pressed together with determination, but Benji could tell that she was also having a lot of fun. Her face wasn't as joyful as when she was on the pitcher's mound, but there was a light to it that made Benji's heart glow.

An hour later, Gabriela and Mami left the studio and rejoined Benji. Benji had never seen Mami look so proud.

"Can you believe that Madame Miyoko said I had the most promise out of any student she had ever taught?" said Gabriela excitedly.

"Of course I can believe it," said Mami. She smiled. "You're my daughter. But more importantly, I've watched you improve your technique over the past couple of weeks. You have the strength and the discipline to do ballet. You work hard at what you love."

"You know, I don't think ballet will ever be more important to me than baseball," said Gabriela. She smiled. "But it might come close, Mami. It might come close."

CHAPTER 8

On the afternoon of the championship game, Benji found Gabriela standing in front of her vanity, looking at her face in the mirror as she held the wig in her hands. Her hair lay in waves against her back.

Benji jumped off the bed and padded up to Gabriela. He nudged her knee. She looked down and smiled at him.

"Hey, Perrito." Gabriela leaned over and scratched the back of Benji's head. Then she set the wig down on top of the vanity and picked up an elastic band. She gathered up her hair and began to wind it in a tight bun.

Benji knew what she was going to do next. He had seen it for the past couple months. Gabriela would tuck her hair under her wig and go play ball.

But he knew that every time she did that, she wasn't being completely herself. He could tell in the way her hands trembled as she swept up her hair that she was nervous. Something big was going to happen today. And Benji wanted Gabriela to be completely herself.

He jumped up and lifted his front paws onto the vanity. Before Gabriela could react, Benji had snatched the wig and was pulling chunks of fake hair out.

"Perrito, no!" cried Gabriela. She tried to grab the wig back, but Benji fled underneath her bed, out of reach.

"I know Coach Stevens is going to let me onto the field as a girl, but I don't know how I'll feel if the other team sees me," Gabriela confessed. "If I look like a boy, I'll feel less scared about this game. They'll tease me if they see I'm a girl, I'm sure of it. Please, Perrito, give me back my wig."

But it was too late. When Benji emerged from under the bed, the wig had been torn clean in half.

Gabriela picked up a piece of the wig. "Perrito! What did you do?" she cried.

Benji woofed. He stared at Gabriela, willing her to see what he saw—a strong, talented young woman who didn't need to hide under a wig to be the best she could be.

Gabriela took a deep breath. "Guess I have no

choice but to be myself today," she said, dumping the wig in the trash.

Benji barked encouragingly. Gabriela sat down next to him. He reached out gently with his teeth and pulled out the elastic keeping her hair back.

Gabriela smiled. "You're right. Maybe I am the best when I'm just myself." She took the elastic from Benji. Instead of pinning her hair up in a bun, though, she pulled it into a long ponytail. It was the same ponytail she had when she had told Brandon that she was thinking about trying out for the team.

When she was done, she plopped a baseball cap on her head and threaded her ponytail through the back. She looked down at Benji. "How do I look?" she asked.

Benji woofed and wagged his tail happily.

"Gracias." Gabriela laughed. "Now let's go win this."

Benji picked up their lucky ball and followed Gabriela out of the bedroom, down the front porch steps, and to the ball field for the final game of the season.

When Gabriela arrived, the Tigers were warming up in the field. The rival team players, the Jackals, were in the visitors' dugout. Benji heard the Jackals' dugout explode in mutters and laughter as Gabriela took her place at the pitcher's mound.

"What's a girl doing out there?" asked a player for the Jackals.

"Get off the field and go paint your nails!" called another Jackal.

Benji saw the color drain from Gabriela's face. Her eyes were full of determination, but her bottom lip began to tremble slightly.

Benji wasn't having any of it. A deep growl erupted from his throat. He dropped the ball and barked loudly at the dugout. He looked at Gabriela, his eyes full of strength and encouragement.

Gabriela took a deep breath. Her lip stopped trembling. "I'll tell you what I'm doing here," she yelled. "I'm Gabriela Maria Elena Lopez, and I'm playing baseball because I'm good at it and the Tigers are gonna win!"

And then, all of a sudden, Brandon, who was at first base, hollered back at the dugout. "That's right! We've got the best pitcher in the state, and you're about to find that out!"

Gabriela gave Brandon a gigantic smile.

"Go, Gabriela!" cheered Mami from the bleachers.

Benji lifted his head and let out a loud howl of encouragement

"Let's get this started!" Gabriela cried as she prepared to pitch. She wound up and threw the ball to the catcher.

"Whoa," muttered the Jackal who had taunted Gabriela. "Did you see how fast that went?"

"Whatever," muttered the second Jackal who had made fun of Gabriela. "She's a girl. It was just a lucky pitch."

"That's not luck—that's skill," replied Gabriela.

When the first Jackal got up to bat, Gabriela gave him a grim smile. Then she unleashed a fastball that blew by the Jackal. He didn't even have time to swing.

"Strike one!" called the ump.

Gabriela's next pitch was a curveball that dipped at the last second into the strike box. Again, the Jackal didn't move the bat an inch. By the time he blinked, the ball had thudded into the catcher's mitt.

"Strike two!" said the ump.

Gabriela wound up and delivered a slider. The Jackal tried to swing, but his timing was too slow.

"Strike three—you're out!" called the ump.

"Yeah, Gabriela!" yelled Coach Stevens. "Atta girl!"

Gabriela grinned. Six pitches and no hits later, the ump called the third out, and the Tigers were up at bat.

The first Tiger struck out. Then Brandon went to bat. He hit a ground ball that got him to second base.

Gabriela was the third at bat. As she walked up to home plate, the pitcher began to snicker. "Just remember," he shouted to her. "This ain't softball.

You actually gotta be good to hit a baseball."

Gabriela paid no attention to him. She bent her knees and lifted the bat behind her. She was ready.

The pitcher wound up and threw the ball. There was a sharp crack, and it disappeared deep into left field.

As the outfielders searched for the ball, Gabriela began to run. She had rounded third by the time the left outfielder had thrown the ball to the pitcher.

"Go home! Go home!" cheered the Tigers.

Gabriel dug her shoes into the dirt and began to run home.

The pitcher zinged the ball to the catcher just as Gabriela approached the plate. She dropped to the ground and slid her leg forward, tapping the base as the catcher's mitt swooped down to tag her.

"Safe!" called the ump.

Benji barked and woofed as the bleachers erupted in cheers.

"Go, Gabriela!" the Tigers fans cried.

"That's my daughter! *Mi hija!*" cried Mami. Her face glowed with pride.

By the top of the ninth, the Tigers were up, 6–5. When Gabriela left the dugout to pitch, Benji could see the Jackals coach whispering to his team. The Jackal who had teased her started to walk toward her.

As Gabriela passed him, the Jackal leaned over and whispered into her ear, "No matter how good you are, guys will always be better than girls at baseball. Always." He gave Gabriela a mean smile and returned to the dugout to grab a bat.

Gabriela's face clouded over. As Benji watched her approach the pitcher's mound, he could tell that she was distracted.

The Jackal sneered at Gabriela from the plate. "Show me what you got, *girl*!" he taunted.

Gabriela threw the ball. The Jackal swung and connected. A few pitches later, Gabriela had made her third out, but not before the Jackal had crossed the home plate to tie the game, 6–6.

As the Tigers got ready for the bottom of the ninth, Coach Stevens gathered the team together for a group huddle. "We just need one more run to win. I know we can do this—especially with the lineup we have." He checked his clipboard. "Alex, you're first at bat. Then Brandon, then Gabriela."

Alex struck out first. Brandon hit a ground ball and got to first base.

"You've got this, Gabriela," said Coach Stevens.

Gabriela walked up to the plate. Her hands were shaking as she held the bat behind her.

The first pitch whistled past her.

"Strike one!" called the ump.

Gabriela shook her head, trying to focus. She readied herself for the next pitch.

The ball came flying, just in the strike zone.

As Gabriela swung, Brandon made a dash for second base.

"Strike two!" called the ump as the catcher whipped the ball to the second baseman.

"You're out!" cried the ump as the baseman tagged Brandon before he could reach the plate.

"It's all up to you!" Coach Stevens told Gabriela.

Benji could see that Gabriela was nervous. He knew he had to do something to help. He ran in front of the bleachers and let out four short howls. He did it again and looked at Mami.

Mami smiled. She knew exactly what Benji was trying to say. "Ga-bri-el-a! Ga-bri-el-a!" she chanted.

The rest of the bleachers chimed in. Their voices filled the park. "Ga-bri-el-a! Ga-bri-el-a!"

Gabriela looked over. She saw her mom cheering her name, along with all the other Tigers fans. Benji was at the front, howling with encouragement.

Gabriela tossed her head. Her hair glinted in the deep afternoon sun. Benji saw a steely look come over her face. She was ready.

The pitch came, a fastball that smoldered through the air.

Gabriela swung. Half a second later, the ball sailed past the pitcher, past the center fielder, and out of sight.

"Home run!" cried Coach Stevens.

As Gabriela rounded the bases, the Jackals took

off their baseball caps and threw them down into the dust. Shouts and happy howls thundered from the bleachers. When she got back to home plate, her teammates scooped her up and threw her in the air.

"Ga-bri-el-a! Ga-bri-el-a!" they cried.

Benji tilted his head back and howled. As he saw Mami run out to embrace her daughter, he knew that Gabriela was going to be all right. She could both do what she loved and be herself, just like him.

He also knew it was time to get going. Benji trotted up to Gabriela and dropped their lucky ball at her feet. She knelt down and he gave her a huge lick on the face.

Gabriela laughed. She hugged him. "You coming home to celebrate?"

Benji whined, and then woofed. He started on his way down the street. When he turned to look back at Gabriela, she was nodding. She picked up the ball and tossed it high.

"*Comprendo, Perrito.* I gotta be me, and you gotta be you. Safe travels—and *muchas gracias*."

Benji leaned back and howled one final time. Then he turned and headed down the road, and on to the new adventures that lay ahead.

FOR MORE **Benji**, CHECK OUT THESE EXCITING STORIES!

Benji
BENJI ON THE ROAD

Benji
BENJI'S FIRST HOLIDAY

Benji
SAVES CAMP

Benji
HOWL-O-WEEN